THE TWENTY-FOUR DAYS
BEFORE CHRISTMAS

MADELEINE L'ENGLE

The Twenty-four Days
Before Christmas

Illustrations by INGA

ARIEL BOOKS · *NEW YORK*

Copyright © 1964 by the Community of the Holy Spirit
Library of Congress catalog card number 64-22125
First printing, 1964
Published simultaneously in Canada
by Ambassador Books, Ltd., Toronto
Manufactured in the United States of America

To the students
of St. Hilda's and St. Hugh's
for their hindrance
and their help

Iт is the first day of December.
The Austin children all jump out of bed before Mother even has
time to say "Wake up!"

Vicky runs to the window to see if it has snowed during the
night. The ground is still bare. The grass has its dull winter
brown and a few leaves blow across it. The trees shake their dark
branches against a grey sky.

"Any snow?" Suzy asks.

Vicky is seven, and three years older than Suzy. She tries to
imitate her big brother John. "Not a smidgin. And the sky isn't
white enough for snow today. But it doesn't matter. It's the first
day of December!"

Everybody in the Austin family is excited on the first day of
December because every day for twenty-four days they will do
something special to prepare for the twenty-fifth day, Christmas
Day, the most joyful day in the whole year.

John is dressed and out of the house before Vicky and Suzy are up. John is ten and he knows more about Christmas and more about everything else than the girls do. John is building a big tree house in the tallest maple tree. John is allowed to ride all alone to the village on his bike. John has a paper route every morning, before school.

Vicky is the middle Austin and she is the ugly duckling. When she has time to think about it and remember it this makes her very sad. She has long pigtails and she's skinny and has long skittery legs like a colt's. But this is a very special year because this year Vicky is going to be The Angel in the Pageant at the church on Christmas Eve. This is the biggest and most wonderful thing that has ever happened to Vicky. She will wear a golden halo and a flowing white costume and the loveliest wings you could possibly imagine. Mother made them.

Suzy is four and she is the baby and if she knew how to sit still she would be the prettiest baby angel imaginable. She has curly hair the color of sunshine. She has great shining eyes that are the purple-blue of the sky just after sunset. She has a rosebud for a mouth, and she isn't skinny a bit. But Suzy couldn't be a baby angel. Suzy cannot be still. And here's a big secret. Suzy isn't going to be the baby for very much longer. This makes

Suzy very happy because a new baby will be even more exciting to have than a new doll.

Vicky and Suzy run down the back stairs to the kitchen just as John comes in from delivering his papers, his cheeks shiny-red as apples from the cold. The dogs come running in after him, barking.

The kitchen is a big wandery room that turns corners and has all kinds of unexpected nooks and crannies. In the dining room end a fire is crackling merrily, and the smell of applewood mingles with the smell of pancakes and maple syrup, and hot chocolate with marshmallows. One of the cats is sleeping, curled up on a cushion in front of the fire. Dr. Austin has already had his breakfast and gone out, because country doctors are very busy.

Mother is waiting for John and Vicky and Suzy with the surprise for the first day of December.

It isn't completely a surprise because each year it's an Advent Calendar, but it's partly a surprise because each year the calendar is new. Advent, John could tell you, is the name for the four weeks of preparation and thought that lead up to Christmas day. This year the calendar comes all the way across the ocean from Denmark. It's a big picture of a village with a beautiful church in the center. Each day one of the children will open one of the little windows to see what surprise picture is waiting behind. On Christmas Eve they will open the doors to the church to see a picture of the infant Jesus. Suzy is the youngest so she opens the

window marked "1." Inside is a baby angel who looks just like Suzy. Suzy wishes she could be an angel in the Pageant like Vicky. But she doesn't say anything. Vicky wishes she could be pretty as an angel like Suzy. But she doesn't say anything.

On the second day of December, everybody, even John, even Dr. Austin when he gets home from the hospital, makes Christmas cookies. Mother says they must make the Christmas cookies early this year.

"We can't be quite sure," she tells the children, "exactly when the new baby will arrive. And I think the baby's going to keep me too busy for Christmas cookies. Babies have a way of doing that."

Vicky was born at the end of November, so Mother didn't make any Christmas cookies the year Vicky was born. "I always seem to spoil things," Vicky thinks sadly. "Please, please, please," she prays, "don't let me spoil the Christmas Pageant. Please make me be a *good* angel."

On the third day of December after John and Vicky get home from school, Mother gets out some wire and empty tin cans and just a few Christmas balls. She takes strong scissors and she cuts the tops and bottoms of the cans in special ways so that they make stars and curlicues. Then they take thread and hang the Christmas

balls and the designs on the wire, and John and Mother balance
it all, and suddenly there is the most beautiful Christmas mobile
you could possibly imagine. John gets on the ladder and hangs the
mobile in the middle of the kitchen ceiling and it turns and twirls
and sparkles in the light.

The next day as usual the children run to the windows and look
for snow, but the ground stays brown, and the trees are dark
against the sky. Each morning as John goes to the garage for his
bike he looks at the big sled, at his father's snowshoes, at the ice
skates, at the skis. But though the wind is damp and chill, it
is not cold enough. The pond has a thin skin of ice, but not

nearly enough for skating, and all that comes from the grey skies is an occasional drizzle that threatens to turn into sleet, not snow.

And the days speed into December. On the fourth day, Dr. Austin puts a big glimmering gold star over the mantelpiece in the living room; and on the fifth day the children tape a Santa Claus and his reindeer up the bannisters of the front stairs. On the sixth day of December they string the merry Norwegian elves across the whole long length of the kitchen windows, and on the seventh day of December a tall golden angel goes above the kitchen mantelpiece. This angel is too stately and too dignified to look like Suzy, and Vicky knows that even in her costume and wings she can never hope to look graceful and beautiful the way the golden angel does. She sighs.

On the eighth day of December, Vicky is late getting home because the rehearsal of the Pageant lasts a whole half-hour longer than usual. It lasts a whole half-hour longer than usual because the director can't get Vicky in a position that satisfies her. Vicky hears the director whisper to the assistant director, "I've never seen a seven-year-old be so awkward or ungraceful, but I suppose we really can't change The Angel now."

Vicky clamps her teeth tight shut in order to keep from crying. "Don't look so sullen, Vicky," the director says. "An angel should be joyful, you know." Vicky nods, but she doesn't dare unclench her teeth. One tear trickles down her cheek, but she doesn't think anybody sees.

When the rehearsal is over the minister drives Vicky home. He says that the Pageant is going to be the most beautiful they've ever had, and that Vicky is going to be a beautiful angel. Vicky doesn't believe him.

The Advent surprise that day is to have the Christmas mugs at dinner, the mugs that look like Santa Claus. But Vicky still feels like crying as she drinks her milk out of the cheerful Santa Claus face, and later on, when everybody has had baths, and they are all ready for bed and standing around the piano singing Advent carols, Vicky has such a big lump in her throat that she can't sing.

Dr. Austin puts his arm around her and says, "What's the matter with my girl?" Two tears trickle out of Vicky's eyes, and she tells him about the rehearsal and what the director has said. He gives Vicky a hug and tells her that Mother will help her to look and move more like an angel. "I think you can be the best angel the Pageant has ever had, but you have to work at it."

On the ninth day of December the Christmas bells are hung from the beams in the living room and Mother works with Vicky so that she can be a better angel. Vicky walks all over the house with a volume of the encyclopaedia on her head. Mother shows

her how to stand with her feet in ballet positions, and how to hold her arms so that they don't look all elbows.

On the tenth day of December Mother gets the cuddly Santa Claus doll out of the attic and tells Vicky and Suzy they can take turns taking it to bed at night. Vicky looks at it longingly and says, "Suzy can have it. May I take the *Shu to Sub* volume of the encyclopaedia to bed with me?"

Mother understands and says yes. "Now put it on your head and try walking up the front stairs and down the back stairs."

Each time Vicky does it she can manage more steps without having to catch the encyclopaedia. Suzy goes to bed with the cuddly Santa Claus doll. Vicky goes to sleep with her cheek against the encyclopaedia, *Shu to Sub*.

On the eleventh day of December Vicky comes home from rehearsal with a shining face because the director beams at her and says, "That was *much* better, Vicky. I think you're going to be all right after all. Now let's try it again. *Good,* Vicky, GOOD!"

Mother gives Vicky a hug, and John says gruffly, "I don't know why anybody ever thought you couldn't do it. I knew you could."

Suzy jumps up and down and says, "What're we going to do for Advent today?"

Mother says, "Let's make a Christmas chandelier." They take the wire mesh lettuce basket and fill it with the Christmas balls that are just a tiny bit broken but not shattered. They hang one of the prettiest, shiniest decorations on the bottom of the lettuce basket, and then Mother and John fit the basket over the front hall light so that it glitters and sparkles with the color of all the Christmas baubles.

Vicky walks up and down the front hall with the encyclopaedia, *Shu to Sub,* on her head, and tries to look at the Christmas chandelier out of the corner of her eye, but when she looks up the encyclopaedia falls off and she catches it just before it lands on the floor.

Now it is the twelfth day of December and not only is there no snow, there is rain. Rain pours in great torrents from the sodden skies and the gutters spout like fountains. After school Mother discovers that they have to make more Christmas cookies because the first batch has been all eaten up! Christmas cookies and carols are good things for a rainy December 12th.

On the thirteenth day of December the skies are all washed clean and the sun is out and there is a rehearsal for the Pageant. The director says, "Vicky dear, you're doing so well that we've decided to give you some lines for the scene where you appear with the shepherds. Do you think you can memorize them?"

Vicky nods happily. It's hard for her to walk without tripping herself up, and to stand still without being all sharp corners and angles, but memorizing things is easy for her.

The director explains, "These are the Angel lines from an old play in the Chester Cycle. The Chester Cycle was a group of plays written a long time ago in England, to be performed in the church in Chester, so we think it's very appropriate for you to say the lines for the early Christmas Eve service. Are you and your family coming for the midnight service, too?"

Vicky nods. "If Suzy takes a long enough nap. But she always does."

"We'll be sorry not to have your mother in the choir this year."

Vicky nods again. "It's because of the new baby, you know."

"Isn't that nice!" the director says. "I wonder if Mother will be in the hospital for Christmas? Now here are your lines, dear. Read them slowly and clearly."

Vicky reads the lines. She reads them slowly and clearly. But she doesn't even hear herself. Mother in the hospital for Christmas! Vicky has known all along that Mother would go to the hospital to have the new baby, just as she did for John and Vicky and Suzy. But not for Christmas Eve! Not for Christmas day!

> "Shepherd, of this sight
> Be not afright," Vicky reads,

"For this is God's night.
To Bethlehem now hie.
There shall ye see and sight
That Christ was born tonight
To save all mankind."

If Mother is in the hospital it won't be Christmas! Christmas is the *whole* family hanging up the stockings, and Daddy reading *The Night Before Christmas* and Saint Luke, and Mother singing

everybody to sleep with carols. What about the stocking presents Christmas morning in Mother's and Daddy's great big fourposter bed? What about running downstairs all together to see the presents under the tree? What about—what about—everything!

Who is going to cook Christmas dinner? Make the stuffing? Roast the turkey? Fix the cranberry? What about putting out cocoa and cookies for Santa Claus the very last thing on Christmas Eve? What about—what about—everything?

"That's very good, dear," the director says. "You speak beautifully. Now read it again, and just a little bit more slowly this time. Do you think you can memorize it for tomorrow?"

Vicky nods numbly. She does everything the director says, but all she can think is, "Mother *has* to be home for Christmas!"

Dr. Austin picks Vicky up after rehearsal that afternoon. As soon as they are safely in the car and the door is shut Vicky demands, "Daddy! Is Mother going to be in the hospital for Christmas?"

He answers quietly, "It's a distinct possibility, Vic."

Vicky shouts, "WHY?"

"Well, the baby's due on the twenty-third of December, honey. But you can never tell exactly when a baby's going to decide to be born. It might be enough earlier so that Mother'll be home for

Christmas. Or it mightn't be until after Christmas. But I'd say the chances are that Mother'll be in the hospital for Christmas. I thought you'd realized that."

"Let's not *have* the baby!" Vicky cries. "I don't *want* the baby, Daddy!"

"Here, here," Dr. Austin says. "That's no way to talk."

"There are enough of us already." Vicky chokes over a sob. "Do we have to have the baby, Daddy?"

"Of course we do," he says. "We all want the baby. This isn't like you, Vicky Austin."

"What about Christmas dinner?" Vicky wails.

"At the last count," Dr. Austin says, "we'd had seventeen invitations for Christmas dinner."

"But we can't go *out* for Christmas dinner!" Vicky cries. "I'd rather have *corn*flakes and have them at home!"

Dr. Austin turns the car up the hill to the house. "I quite agree with you, Vicky. I've turned down all the invitations. If Mother's in the hospital I think you and John and Suzy and I can manage to cook Christmas dinner, don't you? And I'll tell you a secret. Mother already has a turkey stuffed and roasted and in the freezer. All we have to do is thaw it and heat it up in the oven."

Vicky gives an exhausted hiccup. "Well. All right. But it

won't be Christmas without Mother. If I'd known Mother wouldn't be here for Christmas I wouldn't have wanted a new baby."

Dr. Austin changes the subject. He's very good about knowing when to do that. "I heard you saying your Angel lines, Vicky. We're all going to be very proud of you on Christmas Eve."

When they get home Mother and John and Suzy are in the kitchen stuffing dates. John shouts, "Vicky! There's snow forecast for tomorrow!"

On the fourteenth day of December three snowflakes fall. Exactly three. Vicky counts them. They fall while the family is out in the woods picking berries and ground pine for Christmas decorations.

On the fifteenth day of December Dr. Austin and John get out the ladder and Mother and Vicky and Suzy untangle the long strings of outdoor lights and they trim the big Norway spruce.

"We're going to do quite a few things a little earlier than usual this year," Dr. Austin says, "because of not knowing just when the baby is going to decide to be born."

At night the Christmas tree shines so brightly that it can be seen all the way from the main road at the bottom of the hill.

And on the fifteenth day of December Mother comes to pick Vicky up after rehearsal and the director says, "I must admit to you, Mrs. Austin, that I was a little unsure of Vicky for the first few rehearsals. She's the youngest Angel we've ever chosen and I wasn't certain she could do it. But now I think she's going to be the very best Angel we've ever had. And she knows her lines perfectly."

One part of Vicky blazes with happiness. But another part thinks sadly, "It won't be Christmas if Mother isn't home."

As they drive away from the church, Mother points to the hilltop where the Austins' big white house perches, and Vicky sees a little triangle of colored lights that is the outdoor Christmas tree.

"Mother!" Vicky says suddenly. "If you're in the hospital you won't be able to see me being The Angel!"

"No, I won't, Vicky."

"But I *want* you to see me!"

"I want to see you, too."

Vicky scowls. "In the olden days people didn't have to go to hospitals to have babies. They had them at home."

"So they did," Mother agrees. "But even if I had the baby at home I couldn't come see you being The Angel."

"Why not?"

"Brand new babies need a lot of attention," Mother says, "and they can't be taken out in the cold. I was pretty tied down at Christmastime the year you were born, Vicky."

"But I was *born!*" Vicky cries. "And you were home for Christmas. You didn't go off and leave John and Suzy alone. Oh. I forgot. Suzy wasn't born. Anyhow, Mother, please couldn't you ask the baby to wait till after Christmas? Or to hurry up and come right now?"

"I can ask," Mother says. "But I wouldn't count on it, Vic. What shall we do today for Advent?"

"Let's make the wreath for the front door," Vicky suggests.

"Good idea. We've got lots of ground pine and berries left over and I saved all the pine cones we gilded and silvered last year. When we get home you can run up to the attic and get them for me."

On the sixteenth day of December John listens to the weather forecast before breakfast and snow is predicted again. The sky has the white look that means it is heavy with snow. John and Vicky are so pleased that they run almost the whole of the mile down the hill to wait for the school bus. A cold raw wind is blowing and they huddle into their parkas. After school Vicky has a rehearsal. This afternoon John has a rehearsal, too, because he is singing in the choir, and this is the first time that the cast of the Pageant and the choir have worked together.

Vicky tries very hard to walk the way she has learned with the encyclopaedia, *Shu to Sub,* and to move her arms as though they were the graceful branches of a tree in spring and not the bare brittle branches of a tree in December. She remembers all her lines in her heart as well as her mind, and Mother has worked with her so that each word rings out clear and pure as a bell. Everybody is pleased with her, and John pounds her on the back and tells her that she's a whiz. The choir director congratulates her and tells her that everybody is going to miss Mother at the midnight service, and Vicky remembers again that Mother probably won't be home for Christmas. John asks the choir director if he thinks it will snow, but the choir director shakes his head. It has turned too cold for snow, he says.

This afternoon the choir director drives them home and stops in for a cup of tea. A big box of holly and mistletoe has arrived from the cousins on the west coast, so John and Dr. Austin hang the mistletoe on one of the beams in the living room.

After the choir director goes they open the day's Christmas cards, because all the family opens them together, taking turns, so that each card can be looked at and admired and appreciated.

John says, "Some people just rip open their cards in the post office. I bet the kids never see them at all. I'm glad we don't do it that way."

"Everybody's different, John," Mother says. "That's what makes people interesting."

"Nobody else I know does something every day during Advent the way we do," John says. "I'm glad we're different. What's our thing for today, Mother?"

"Oh, I think the holly and the mistletoe's plenty," Mother says. "Get the table set, Vicky. It's time to eat."

The days towards Christmas fly by, and still there is no snow. And no baby. And each day Vicky is happier about being The Angel.

On the seventeenth of December they hang the doll angels all over the house, and on the eighteenth they put the Christmas candle in the big kitchen window. On the nineteenth the children make their Christmas cards. They use colored paper and sparkle and cutouts from last year's Christmas cards.

On the twentieth day of December they put up the crèche. This is one of the most special of all the special things that happen before Christmas. Over the kitchen counter is a cubby hole with two shelves. Usually mugs are kept in the bottom shelf, and the egg cups and the pitcher that is shaped like a cow on the top shelf. But now Mother makes places for these in one of the kitchen cabinets. On the top shelf goes the wooden stable and the holy family and the shepherds. Tiny wax angels fly over the stable. A dove sits on the roof. The ox and the ass and all the barnyard animals are put in, one by one, everybody taking turns. One of the shepherds carries a lamb. There is even a tiny pink pig from a barnyard set someone once gave John. There is a sheepdog and a setting hen and a grey elephant the size of the pig. Some people might think the elephant doesn't belong, but the year that Vicky was born Daddy gave him to John, and John didn't think he ought to be left out. He's been there ever since, and nobody in the Austin family thinks he looks peculiar there at all.

On the bottom shelf are the wise men and their camels and their page. The children make a hill out of cotton, which is a little hard to balance the camels on, but it really looks as though the train of camels was climbing up a long weary road to the Christ Child. On Twelfth Night they will have finished their journey and will join the shepherds and the animals in the stable.

Last of all Daddy puts the star up above the stable and fixes the light behind it. Then John runs around and turns off every other light in the house and all that you can see is the lovely light from the star shining on the stable and The Holy Family and the angels and the animals. The elephant stays meekly in the shadows.

On the twenty-first day of December Dr. Austin and the children go out into the woods to get the Christmas tree. Mother stays home, because she is feeling tired, but everybody else tramps through the woods, including the dogs and the cats. Suzy is the one who finds the perfect tree, just the right shape for the living room, with beautiful firm branches all round. Dr. Austin and John take turns sawing, and everybody helps carry the tree home because it is a tall one, and heavy.

Dr. Austin says, "Tomorrow is Sunday so we'll trim the tree a little ahead of time to get it ready for Santa Claus and to make sure Mother's here to help."

John asks, "You really don't think the baby's going to wait till after Christmas, Daddy?"

"I rather doubt it," his father says. "Now, children, we'll put the tree carefully in the garage until tomorrow."

That night Vicky wakes up, very wide awake. She knows that it isn't anywhere near morning because the light is still on in her parents' bedroom. After a few minutes Vicky gets up, softly, so as not to waken Suzy. She puts on her bathrobe and slippers and tiptoes downstairs to the kitchen. The dogs come pattering out to meet her, wagging their tails. One of the cats meows at the head of the cellar stairs. Vicky puts her fingers to her lips and says, "Shh! Everybody go back to sleep."

It isn't quite dark in the kitchen because the embers in the fireplace are still glowing. Mother and Daddy must have gone up to bed just a little while ago. Vicky tiptoes over to the crèche, climbs on one of the kitchen stools, and turns on the light behind the star. She stays there on the stool and looks at the nativity scene for a long time. Then she reaches in, very, very gently, and brings out the manger and the Christ Child. The manger is made of wood and straw and the little Lord Jesus is made of wax. He is very tiny but his eyes seem to shine and his lips to smile.

Vicky says to him, very softly, "I don't want Mother to be in the hospital for Christmas. I want her to be home." Then she says, "I'd give anything if she could be home." Very carefully Vicky puts the little straw manger back. "If there were something I could give to keep Mother home for Christmas I'd give it. But I don't have anything to give!" she says loudly. Too loudly. She puts her finger to her lips and says, "Shhh!" to herself. She whispers fiercely to the baby. "What can I give? I don't *have* anything."

She thinks, "I wouldn't mind giving up the new baby, but Mother and Daddy wouldn't like that. Anyhow the new baby isn't for me. He's for everybody."

She looks and looks at the little Christ Child on his bed of straw. Suddenly her eyes widen, and she shakes her head hard as though trying to get rid of the thought that has come to it. "No. No," she whispers. She looks away from the baby Jesus to the angels, to the dove on the roof, to the pig and the elephant standing meekly together outside the stable. She folds her hands together and breathes hard. She closes her eyes tight. "Being The Angel is the most important thing in the world to me. I guess it's the only thing I have to give. I'm not trying to make a bargain with You or anything, truly I'm not, but if I ask You for a Christmas present, shouldn't I give You a present, too? But You'll have to show me how. I can't just go to rehearsal on Monday and say I won't be The Angel, because there isn't time for anybody else to learn it all. That would be letting everybody in the Pageant down, and Mother and Daddy say you mustn't let people down. I don't know how to give up being The Angel, but if You'll show me how, and if it will keep Mother home for Christmas, I'll do it."

She opens her eyes. Is the baby Jesus still smiling? The light from the star shines over the holy family and the animals and the shepherds. It shines on the kings and the camels climbing the cotton hill to Bethlehem. Everything looks quiet and peaceful and beautiful. All at once Vicky feels very sleepy. She climbs down from the stool and tiptoes across the kitchen and up the stairs. She gets into bed and pulls up the covers. And falls asleep.

On the twenty-second day of December when everybody is home from Sunday school and church Mother makes hamburgers and milkshakes for lunch because that is the quickest thing to have. Vicky and Suzy help with the dishes and Mother puts on a

Christmas carol record, and everybody sings loudly, *O Come, O Come, Emmanuel*. Dr. Austin and John bring in the tree from the garage and set it firmly in a bucket of wet sand. The big boxes of Christmas decorations are brought down from the attic. First of all Dr. Austin gets on the ladder and he and John put on the lights, and the angel at the top of the tree. This angel is in white

with sparkling wings. It is this angel Mother has copied for Vicky's costume. Vicky watches while her father carefully puts the angel at the top of the tree. She remembers the night before. She doesn't want to give up being The Angel. And even if she *did* want to, she doesn't see how it can possibly be done without upsetting the Pageant and that wouldn't be right. But more than anything she wants Mother home for Christmas.

She screws up her face in concentration and thinks, "If You'll show me how to give up being The Angel without hurting anybody else I'll do it, as long as it'll keep Mother home for Christmas."

Mother looks at her and says, "What's the matter, Vicky?"

Vicky unscrews her face and shakes her head. "Nothing. May I put on some of the breakable ones this year?"

Suzy is given the unbreakable ornaments that go on the lowest branches of the tree. Mother smiles and hands Vicky a beautiful little glass horn that really makes a sound. Vicky blows it and Suzy has to blow it, too. Everybody works together and soon the tree is shimmering with beauty. Everybody sings loudly with the carol: *"Hark, the Herald Angels Sing!"*

Vicky puts a gold glass bell that tinkles gently on the highest branch she can reach. When the last decoration is hung from the tree and everybody exclaims (as usual) that it is the most beautiful tree *ever,* John runs around, and turns off every light in the house, so that the Christmas tree shines alone in the darkness. They all stand very still, looking at it. Everything is peaceful and happy.

Vicky has even forgotten for a little while about The Angel.

On the twenty-third day of December when Vicky goes to the church for dress rehearsal it begins to snow. All the children in the Pageant clap and shout with glee and keep running to the doors to look at the great feather flakes fluttering from a soft fluffy sky. Finally the director gets cross at them and orders everyone inside.

In the Sunday School rooms several mothers are helping the children get into costume. Vicky is in hers early. The mother who helped her get dressed says, "Vicky dear, if you stand around here in this mob your wings are going to get crushed. Go sit quietly in the back of the church until we're ready to start the dress rehearsal."

Vicky goes carefully through the big doors and walks halfway down the nave. The church has been transformed with pine boughs and candles. The candles won't be lit until the performance of the Pageant the next afternoon and again for the midnight service, but there is a spotlight shining on the manger. The girl who is to be Mary comes and stands beside Vicky. She is a high school senior and very, very grown up. She wears a pale blue gown and a deep blue robe. She drops one hand lightly on Vicky's shoulder. She says, "Some of us thought it was funny, such a little kid being chosen for The Angel, and at first we thought you were going to be awful and ruin everything. But now I think you're going to be the best thing in the Pageant. I honestly do." Then Mary goes and sits by the manger. She sits very still, her head bowed. She doesn't seem like a high school senior any

more. She seems to belong in Bethlehem. Vicky slips into one of the pews. She is no longer thinking of being The Angel or not being The Angel. She is caught up in the quiet of the blue-robed figure by the manger.

Then it is time for the rehearsal to begin, and everything is hustle and bustle again. The choir in their red cassocks and white surplices lines up for the processional. Vicky is shown into the corner behind the organ from where she will make her first entrance.

The organ starts. The choir marches in. Vicky, bearing a lily, appears before Mary.

Everything goes smoothly. Vicky moves as though she had the encyclopaedia, *Shu to Sub,* on her head. Her arms are curves instead of angles. Her face is shining as though it had been lighted from within. Her words to the shepherds fall as clear as bells. At the final tableau she stands by the manger, and joy shines through her.

After the choir has recessed and the spotlight has faded on the nativity scene, the director congratulates everybody. "It was beautiful, just beautiful!" she says. The mothers who helped with the costumes and stayed to watch echo her, "Beautiful! Beautiful!"

The director gives Vicky a special smile. "Vicky, you were just perfect! Don't change one single thing. Tomorrow for the performance do it just exactly the way you did today."

Vicky nods solemnly. It looks as though she weren't going to be told how to give up being The Angel.

Dr. Austin picks John and Vicky up on his way home from the office. It is still snowing, great heavy flakes. The ground is already white. Dr. Austin says, "I'm glad I got those new snow tires after all."

John says, "You see, Dad, we *are* going to have a white Christmas."

When the children wake up on Christmas Eve morning they run to the windows. Not only is the ground white but they cannot even see the road. Mother says the snow plough went through at five o'clock so the farmers could get the milk out, but the road has already filled in again.

The children eat breakfast quickly, put on snow suits, and

run out to play. The snow is soft and sticky, the very best kind for making snow-men and building forts. They spend the morning making a Christmas snow-man, and start a fort around him. John is quite good at cutting blocks out of the snow like an Eskimo. They aren't nearly finished when Mother calls them in to lunch.

After lunch Suzy says, "I might as well go upstairs and have my nap and get it over with." Suzy is very business-like about things like naps. Mother looks a little peculiar, but she doesn't say anything, and Suzy goes upstairs to bed. Mother lights the kitchen fire and sits down in front of it to read to Vicky and John. They are just settled and comfortable when the phone rings. Mother answers it. She says, "Yes, I was afraid of that. . . . Of course. . . . They'll be disappointed, but they'll have to understand." She hangs up and turns to the children.

"What's the matter?" John asks.

Mother says, "The Pageant's been called off because of the blizzard, and so has the midnight service."

"But WHY!?" John demands.

Mother looks out the window. "How do you think anybody could travel on our road, John? We're completely snowed in. The road men are concentrating on keeping the main roads open but all the side roads are unusable. That means that more than half the village is snowed in just like us. I'm sorry about The Angel, Vicky. I know it's a big disappointment to you, but remember that lots of other children are disappointed, too."

Vicky looks over at the crèche, then back at Mother, and says, "Well, I guess lots of worse things could happen." She thinks, "This isn't exactly how I thought I'd give up being The Angel, but as long as it keeps Mother home for Christmas I guess I don't mind. Too much."

"You're a good girl to be so philosophical," Mother says.

John says, "Anyhow, it looks as though the baby were going to wait till after Christmas."

Mother answers, "Let's hope so."

John presses his nose against the window until the pane steams up. "How is Daddy going to get home?"

It seems to Vicky that Mother looks anxious as she says, "I must admit I'm wondering that myself."

"But it's Christmas Eve!" John says. "He *has* to get home!"

All Mother says is, "Daddy'll do the best he can."

Vicky marches angrily up to the crèche. She doesn't speak aloud but her thoughts are so noisy she's afraid they'll be heard. "I said I'd give up being The Angel if *Mother* could be home for Christmas. I didn't mean anything about *Daddy* not being here."

When it begins to get dark Suzy wakes up, all pink from sleep, and comes hurrying downstairs. She is very cross when Mother tells her that the Pageant and the midnight service have been called off, so she needn't have slept so long after all.

"I wanted to see Vicky be The Angel," she says.

Mother answers, "We all did, Suzy."

Suzy stamps. "I'm *mad* at the old blizzard."

Mother laughs. "That's not going to stop the snow. And remember you've been looking for snow every day. Now you've got it."

John lights the candle in the window and flicks the switch that turns on the outdoor Christmas tree and the switch that turns on the light over the garage. Then all the children go to the window and look out. The only way you can tell where the road

used to be is by the five little pines at the edge of the lawn, and by the birches across the road. The outdoor Christmas tree is laden with snow and the lights shine through and drop small bright pools of color on the white ground. The great flakes of snow are still falling, soft and starry against the darkness.

"I guess Daddy'll have to spend the night at the hospital," John says.

Mother comes to the window and looks out over the children's heads. "No car can possibly get up that road."

Suzy asks, "What're we going to have for dinner?"

Mother turns from the window. "I think I'll just take hamburger out of the freezer so we won't have any leftovers with turkey coming tomorrow."

Vicky stays by the window. She is saying to herself over and over again, "Let Daddy get home. Please let Daddy get home," even though she knows that Mother is right and a car couldn't possibly get up the road. But she goes on. "I didn't mean it this way about The Angel. It isn't Christmas without *both* Mother and Daddy. Please let Daddy get home. Please let Daddy get home."

Then, just as the words begin to get jumbled in her mind, she sees something in the wide expanse of snow, somewhere near where the curve of the road ought to be. It is a light. "Mother! John! Suzy!" she calls. They all come running to the window.

"It's a flashlight," John says.

"Snowshoes!" Mother cries. "John, run to the garage and see if Daddy took his snowshoes!"

John hurries out the kitchen door and in a minute he's back, grinning happily. "They're gone."

The light comes closer and closer and soon they can see that it is Dr. Austin, his head and shoulders covered with snow. His

snowshoes move steadily and regularly over the white ground. The children run tumbling out to the garage and fling their arms about him. The dogs jump up on him and bark in greeting.

"Whoa!" he says. "Let me get my snowshoes off!" He hands the snowshoes to John, who hangs them up. Then he stamps his feet and shakes, and snow tumbles off him. The dogs dash out into the snow, come whirling back into the garage, and shake off even more snow. "Come along," he says. "Let's get in out of the cold."

When they get indoors Daddy kisses Mother. She leans her head against his shoulder. "I was afraid you wouldn't be able to get home."

He says, "You didn't think I'd leave you now, did you?" He puts another log on the fire. Outdoors the snow is still falling. Indoors it is warm and cozy. The star lights up the little stable with the baby Jesus lying on his bed of straw. All the Christmas decorations sparkle. John goes into the living room and turns on the Christmas tree lights so that there is the beauty of the Christmas tree indoors and the beauty of the Christmas tree outdoors in the falling snow. Vicky looks at the angel on top of the indoor Christmas tree and doesn't even sigh.

Everybody helps Mother get dinner. When they are almost through eating Mother gives a funny little gasp, looks at Daddy, and says, "How are you going to get me to the hospital?"

Dr. Austin laughs. "Upstairs is as far as I'm going to get you tonight." He gets up from the table, saying, "Children, I'm going to ask you to do the dishes and clean up the kitchen. Then put a kettle full of water on to boil. Blizzards don't ask anybody when they should come and neither do babies."

The father and mother go upstairs.

"What about dessert?" Suzy asks.

"If you're really interested in dessert I'll get you some ice cream out of the freezer," John says.

After all Suzy is a very little girl. She eats a large bowl of ice cream.

When the kitchen is all cleaned up Dr. Austin comes down stairs. He carries the Christmas stockings and tells the children to hang them carefully at the living room fireplace. "You'd be staying up late tonight anyhow," he says, "so please just be good. Vicky, keep that kettle hot for me, and put the cats down in the cellar for the night."

The snow beats against the windows. The wind rattles the shutters. In spite of her nap Suzy gets sleepy and curls up on the living room sofa.

Vicky goes to the stove. "I'd better make the cocoa to put on the mantelpiece with the cookies for Santa Claus."

"Make enough for us while you're at it," John says.

They drink two, three cups of cocoa. They tiptoe out to the store room where they have hidden their presents for Mother and Daddy and put them under the tree. Time seems to stretch out and out and Dr. Austin doesn't come back downstairs. The dogs lie in front of the fire and snore. Suddenly one pricks up his ears. Vicky and John listen, but they don't hear anything. At the top of the cellar stairs a cat meows. The dog sits up and raises his head. His tail thumps against the floor.

Then Vicky and John do hear something, unmistakable, loud and clear. A cry. A baby's cry.

In a little while Dr. Austin comes bounding down the stairs. He is beaming. "You have a little brother, children!" he says.

He takes the kettle and hurries back up the stairs, calling, "You can come up in a few minutes. Wait."

The baby cries again, a lusty yell.

Vicky goes to the crèche. The light from the star shines down on the stable. The elephant and the pig seem to have moved in closer. The baby lies in his bed of straw.

"Listen," John says, holding up his hand. Across the fields comes the sound of the clock in the church steeple striking midnight. "Let's wake up Suzy," John says, "and tell her."

Suzy sleeps soundly and it takes them a long time to wake her up properly. By the time she realizes what has happened Dr. Austin has come back downstairs. He says, "You can come up now, for just a minute, children. But Mother's tired and the baby's asleep, so be very quiet."

They tiptoe up the stairs and into the big bedroom. Mother is lying in the big bed and smiling. In the crook of her arm is a little bundle. The children tiptoe closer. The bundle is a baby. His face is all puckered and rosy. His eyes are closed tight. He has a wisp of dampish hair. He has a tiny bud of a mouth. One little fist is close to his cheek. The children stand and look and look. They are too excited and awed to speak.

Mother says, "Isn't he beautiful?" And they all nod.

Daddy says, "All right. Time for bed, everybody." They go into the girls' room, go to the window, and stand looking out.

The snow has stopped. The ground is a great soft blanket of white broken by dark lines of trees and the gay colors of the outdoor tree. The sky is dark and clear and crusted with stars.

One star is brighter and more sparkling than any of the others.

"The Christmas star," Vicky whispers. Its light seems to shine right down into her heart.